George Raukin

A dream of empire

George Raukin

A dream of empire

ISBN/EAN: 9783337175672

Printed in Europe, USA, Canada, Australia, Japan

Cover: Foto ©Andreas Hilbeck / pixelio.de

More available books at **www.hansebooks.com**

A DREAM OF EMPIRE

A DRAMA

IN FIVE ACTS

BY

NOBODY-IN-PARTICULAR.

SAN FRANCISCO:

FRANCIS, VALENTINE & CO. PRINTERS 517 CLAY STREET.

1883.

TO ANY HUMBLE LOVER OF THIS COUNTRY,
WHO HAS A PIOUS HATRED FOR EVERY-
THING THAT SMACKS OF ROYALTY,
THIS PLAY IS DEDICATED.

DRAMATIS PERSONÆ.

General Mentor Brandon (afterward Ulysses I).
Senator Clarence Wolford (afterward Lord Wolford, and Emperor).
Senator McDonald, } Friends of Brandon and Wolford.
Senator Maxwell, }
Randemer (afterward Duke of Erie).
Starlow (afterward Earl of California).
Wallace Minnard,
General Shelborn, } Generals in U. S. Army.
General Pitsborough, }
A Captain.
An Admiral.
An Aid-de-Camp.
An Old Man.
Messengers.
Guards.
Servant.
Catherine Minnard (Wife of Wallace Minnard).
Miriam Wolford (Wife of Clarence Wolford).
Leonora Minnard (Daughter of Wallace Minnard).
Alexander the Great,
Cæsar,
Louis XIV.,
Frederic the Great,
Peter the Great,
Napoleon I., } Apparitions in the Dream.
An Egyptian King,
Hannibal,
Washington,
Catherine II.,
Cleopatra,
Neptune,
Mars,
Mercury,
Morpheus,
Oneiros,
Ikelos,
Phobetor,
Three Fatui. } Appearing in the Dream.
Minerva,
Venus,
Themis,
Eirene,
Hestia,
Fortuna,
Fama,
Nymphs,
Ghosts of Woman and Child.
Ghosts of Man and Woman.
Ghost of Miriam Wolford.
Lords, Ladies, Conspirators, Officers, Soldiers and other attendants.

The date of the play is supposed to be 1884–5.

A DREAM OF EMPIRE.

ACT I.

SCENE 1—*New York. A room in Minnard's House. Brandon in room.*

Brandon. This waiting, this uncertainty weighs heavily upon me, and I am overloaded with impatience. O, I am sick and tired of it all, and wish it ended, or that it never had begun. Truly does he who climbs the pinnacle of earth's dizzy heights take the trouble with the honor. What crazy attribute of mind is that which makes us mount some towering rugged peak, 'midst glaciers and falling avalanches, round the steep edges of high hanging cliffs, suspended here by treacherous holdings over a thousand feet of death, worn out, half dead, the summit reached—for what? To look down—nothing else. To this no less a relative than a brother is that insane impulse which drives me, like a slave scourged by his master's lashes, to again attempt the ascent of the highest point on this great nation's honor. Twice have I toiled to that stupendous height. Others have done the same. Aye, there it is; for 'tis a sickly ambition that rests contented even balanced with another. And yet I never found an easy resting-place on that high peak. Fool that I am, to again attempt the perilous position! Yet I would do it—yes, I would do it, though an earthquake shook it from its base, and all the thunders, lightnings and storms of heaven and earth and hell were on its top turned loose! I am abashed at my enthusiasm. Quiet, my thoughts! Here Wolford comes at last.

Enter CLARENCE WOLFORD.

Good evening, Wolford. I have been waiting for you for some time.

Wol. Good evening, General. I am sorry to have kept you waiting, but it was not my idleness that did so.

Bra. I beg your pardon, Clarence, if in my voice there was the slightest unkind accent.

Wol. Think not of that; it was my own impatience.

Bra. O, Wolford, you have done so much for me——

Wol. Tut! no more of that. I have just come from McDonald and Maxwell. Brandon, if the Almighty ever made two noble men they are the twain.

Bra. Who with yourself do constitute the trinity. More of manhood in them would have burst their mortal spheres.

Wol. They are made up of the attributes which make men men.

Bra. Why, so they are. Such attributes are not many, they are rather rich. Supreme o'er all is the iron quality of friendship. Possession of it makes a man a giant. No miser, libertine or traitor ever had it. And next I think the character of bravery is most important. Still, these two attributes alone make but a soft and easy-bending man; but when they're tempered with cool, steady, clear-eyed caution, the trinity of manhood is complete.

Wol. Ah! now I think thou hast been playing the maiden with thyself before a mirror, that thou shouldst see so plainly the attributes of true manhood.

Bra. Rather I have been thinking of my three good friends—yourself, McDonald, and brave, fearless Maxwell. But pardon me, Wolford. You have come from the convention. What news bring you?

Wol. None that's too bad to tell, nor yet too good to keep.

Bra. Then tell me.

Wol. The situation is unchanged. As you might expect, your friends stand by you in solid phalanx, while the mongrel curs that form the opposition are broken into a score of howling packs.

Bra. I have no fear of the desertion of my followers. I never yet betrayed a friend, nor had a friend betray me.

Wol. No. The fear is, that the opposition may unite. Those half-bred puppies; those snarling, cowardly yellow dogs! What could they do in a great campaign, like that before us, with their sniveling and driveling and sanctimonious hypocrisy! What a heavenly lot they are, with their great calf-eyed looks!

Bra. Hold, Wolford! I fear you are too severe on our enemies. But Bradberry and his men? They showed signs of weakness once; what are they doing now?

Wol. Still against you. They form one pack, and their particular howl is: "Civil service reform!" I have no communication with them. But Maxwell told me, when I left, that their disease was not so serious as at first, and that a promise of a few fat offices would cure their mania for reform and bring them over.

Bra. What answer made you to him?

Wol. That if the worse came to the worse, to promise the dogs what they wanted.

Bra. I do not like that! If I should be nominated and elected, I would enter office weighed down with a lot of howling idiots.

Wol. Nonsense! What signifies a promise made under such circumstances? It's like an agreement with a highwayman, to return with more coin, provided he won't murder you outright.

Bra. But no man ever knew me to break a promise.

Wol. My good Brandon, have you made any promises?

Bra. Did you not say you told Maxwell to promise them what they wanted, which will be nothing short of a cabinet office?

Wol. Well, yes, so I did; but that was my agreement, not your's, nor was it made with your knowledge or consent.

Bra. He who accepts the benefit of an unauthorized agent's act must assume the responsibility. Wolford, I will not have my enemies for my counselors.

Wol. Well, sir, since your opposition is so pronounced, I presume the promise can be withdrawn. I shall attend to it instantly. [Takes his hat to go.]

Enter Servant, with letter.

Ser. A letter for Mr. Wolford. (*Exit Servant.*)

Wol. (Reading.) "Bradberry and his men came over under promise of the Treasury, and Brandon was nominated on the three-hundredth ballot, amid the most tremendous applause. The scene is wild beyond description. Everybody crazy. Maxwell." Do you hear that? I congratulate you, Mr. President.

Bra. But, Wolford, it was the promise by which I succeeded.

Wol. To hell with the promise! It was the poison which killed the dogs. Success, not promises is the aim of life, and the means to be employed are those which will effect the end. Success never yet crowned human efforts by the use of means alone of which the Bible would approve.

Bra. Ah! Wolford, how much I am your debtor.

Wol. (aside). Now will I play the hypocrite myself a little. (Aloud) No, you are not my debtor. But if you are, here I forgive the debt, and in the future I shall try to make you owe me more; it is so pleasant to forgive. This only do I ask for pay, that I may serve you better.

Bra. It were far better that I were your servant. But, Wolford, fate may place me in a position where I shall need a helper, greater far than I. Such you shall be, Clarence, if you will. Thou art my genius, my bright star, my sun by which alone I shine. Freely do I confess it—when thou art gone, then am I black nothingness.

Wol. (aside). Then shall I cease to be your sun right quickly. (Aloud) Brandon, if thou art my friend, never again make mention of my services to thee. Love is a term which ill defines the feelings of man for man. It is a womanish word, and my attachment for thee is of a stronger, deeper and more lasting kind. From it springs all that I have ever done, or shall do for thee. 'Tis natural as nature. I neither make it, nor if I would, could I unmake it; nor claim I credit for it. So let it rest, a theme for silent thought, not speech. Now to other business, Mr. President——

Bra. Not so soon, Mr. President. The tree has only bloomed. E'er the fruit's gathered it must go through fierce storms and stand the stings of small yet venomous insects. A hard battle is before us.

Wol. In which millions will rally to the standard of the man who carried the stars and stripes through the fire and tempest of rebellion, made every man in America a freeman, and saved the Nation's honor unspotted.

Enter McDonald *and* Maxwell.

Hail, Senators! You should have garlands on your brows.

McD. Good evening, General; the fight is over and the battle's won.

Bra. Did ever man have three such friends as these?

Enter MINNARD, RANDEMER, STARLOW, GENERAL SHELBORN *and others.*

Min. All our congratulations, General. The great news has reached the street, and in every mouth there is but one word and that is Brandon. [They gather around Brandon and congratulato him.]

Ran. Success is now assured.

Star. (to Ran.) I pledge a million to his election.

Ran. (to Star. and Gen. Shel.) And I, double that amount to keep him President forever!

Shel. Tut! That sounds like treason, Randemer.

Ran. Well, General, call it what you may—treason or patriotism —it's what I'm in for.

Shel. It's what cuts men's heads off, too.

Ran. (to Shel. and Star.) The day for cutting men's heads off is passed. We need a man at the head of this great government who will give stability to it; who will put down communism and keep it down, too, and who will protect our property from rabbles. Brandon's the man.

[*While* RANDEMER, SHELBORN *and* STARLOW *have moved to one part of the stage*, MAXWELL, MCDONALD *and* WOLFORD *have moved to another.*]

Max. (to Wolford). How did he take the promise to Bradberry?

Wol. He didn't like it; or, at any rate, pretended not to.

McD. Well, it was our last chance. The next ballot would have nominated the Half-breed.

Min. [Passing over to Mc., Max. and Wol.] Welcome, Senators, to my house! You have accomplished a grand work to-day!

Enter CATHERINE MINNARD, LEONORA, *and other ladies.*

Cath. If there should need a pardon for our interruption—not to say, intrusion—let it be woman's curiosity. What means this look of joy on each man's face, if not that our great friend is nominated?

Min. Truly has woman's curiosity been answered by woman's intuition. Rightly judged, my dear; the General has been nominated.

Cath. And a dozen pretty speeches made to him, already! What is there left for me to say? Well, General, I will assume to merit of them all, and so tender my congratulations.

Bra. I thank you, madam.

[MCD. *and* MAX. *have moved away from* WOL. *to* BRA. CATH. *moves over to Wol., and other ladies and gentlemen remain about* BRANDON, *conversing with him.*]

Cath. (To Wol.) Good evening, Senator. How glad I am to see you.

Wol. Thank you, Catherine. You look a queen to-night.

Cath. There is but one thing mars my happiness.

Wol. And were it possible I could remove it, what would I not do?

Cath. Did you mean by that that I should tell you what it is?

Wol. If so it please you, I shall gladly listen, Catherine.

Cath. I have heard it said that, at great intervals of time, Dame Nature giveth birth to a great man in each particular line of human calling; then resteth. If such be true, there is one here who is her last great gift of statesmen; one far more fit to be a ruler than any king that ever graced a throne.

Wol. Know you such a man? Your description fits none of my acquaintances.

Cath. The modesty of true greatness never lets it know itself.

Wol. Ah, Catherine, such great flattery is cruelty!

Cath. Nay, Clarence; when thou art in my mind my tongue is but the instrument of honest thoughts. Brandon will be President. It should be thee! He may be great; but thou, thou art supreme.

Wol. O, that I could find words to tell thee of my deep devotion to thee, Catherine! But list! I fear we shall attract attention. Change the subject.

Cath. Thy subject shall be mine as I thy subject am.

Wol. Then tell me, madam, who is that pretty young lady over there—she with the face all suffused with modest blushes?

Cath. Do you not know my daughter, Senator—my daughter Nora? Now I think, you have not seen her for some years. She has been away at school and in that time mayhaps she has escaped your memory.

Wol. Now I remember her. I knew her when she was a little girl, but she has quite outgrown my recollection. She is very pretty. May I not have the pleasure of her acquaintance?

Cath. Certainly. She is only little past sixteen and scarce has put aside her childish ways. Being her mother I would repress my thoughts to one less dear, but to you I'll say she is the sweetest and most confiding girl I ever knew.

Wol. And one more lovely never filled my eyes. She is worthy such a mother.

Cath. Nora, dear, come here. [Nora crosses to Catharine and Wolford.] Nora, this is Senator Wolford.

Nora. I am proud to meet one whom the nation so much delights to honor.

Cath. After this hard day's work perhaps our friends would not refuse a little luncheon.

Min. A good idea. Without more ceremony let us find it.

[*Exeunt all except Wolford and Nora.*

Wol. [Taking Nora's hand.] Stay a little, my young friend, and let me tell you how keenly I feel the pleasure of your acquaintance. You are so pure and innocent, so unspotted by the sins of this great world. O, Leonora, if I could only live forever in so pure a presence!

Nora. But is it so, that this is such a bad, bad world? To me it has ever been a very, very bright and good one. I never yet have known what sorrow is.

Wol. Your path has been all roses; you have never known the thorny side of life.

Nora. Oh! no, sir, not from my earliest infancy. In my little childhood days I never felt a greater sorrow than that occasioned by the breaking of a doll; and well I remember how quickly even that was changed to joy when papa came and kissed away the tear and brought me a better doll. For my teacher, till I came to girlhood, I had the sweetest lady in the world—my mamma. How I love her! O, sir, you can never know how good and kind and gentle mamma is! And then I went to the Convent of Saint Josephine, where mamma came frequently to visit me, and now I have returned to find myself in a flowery kingdom of love and gentle kindness.

Wol. And you have grown up to be the sweetest flower in all this flowery kingdom.

Nora. O, Senator! I fear you flatter me.

Wol. No, no, my little Nora. To flatter is a thing that I am never guilty of. If I spoke plainly and enthusiastically, it was because the purity of your life and your beauty so bade me speak.

Nora. (Aside.) I wonder if this is but common talk. How wonderfully this great man impresses me!

Wol. (Aside.) Did ever any one see such innocence! (Aloud.) Gentle, loving Leonora, let me give thee my best wishes. May thy pathway be all roses, 'till the end of life. May thy beauty grow each day, and none but friends about thee be.

Nora. Oh, sir! oh, oh, sir! How good you are to wish me all this happiness. What may I wish you in return? What do you most want? To be President?

Wol. What do I most want, little one? To be President? No. You have it in your power to give me what I most wish for. Will you do it?

Nora. I, Senator? Why, I would give you anything in my power.

Wol. It is your friendship, Nora—the friendship of a pure, innocent girl. Will you give it?

Nora. Yes, gladly.

Wol. Swear it. Hold up your right hand. You do solemnly swear that you will always be my friend. (Kisses her forehead.) The bargain is sealed. We will be friends forever. Now let us go to luncheon. [*Exeunt.*]

SCENE 2.—*The Same. A street in front of a Hotel. A crowd of Citizens calling for Brandon. A band playing. The city illuminated.*

Enter BRANDON *on balcony, when three cheers are given by citizens.*

Bra. MY FELLOW COUNTRYMEN: I should be little short of dumb, if I were to suppose for one moment that this homage was paid to me. I know full well that it is not me, as a man, you so much honor, but the President-elect of the greatest country the sun of heaven ever shown upon. [Applause and cheers.] I never made a speech in my life and could hardly begin now. So I will only say, I am profoundly grateful to you all for the confidence you have shown in me, in selecting me your President. And I promise you, one and all, that you shall never have cause to regret it. With this much I bid you all good-night. [Loud cheers and music.]

[*Exeunt.*]

Enter WOLFORD, MAXWELL *and* McDONALD.

Wol. Was ever such enthusiasm seen before, for any President?

Max. Why, the country has gone wild over him.

McD. No better time than this will ever come.

Wol. His vote was all but unanimous.

Max. Every return, as it comes in, increases his majority.

McD. [to Wal.] You broached the subject to Randemer and Minnard?

Wol. Yes, and they are all panting for it.

Max. I spoke to Stanlow, or rather, after the first suggestion he did the speaking.

Wol. Oh, you can depend on all of that class. And I honestly believe the country wants him. We must have General Shelborn and the army. In any *coup d'etat* we need the army.

Max. Leave that to me. We are particular friends. Ambition cuts no small part in his make up, conceal it as he may.

Wol. Well, be with me to-morrow evening, for you know we banquet Brandon at my house. Then we'll see what sort of stuff the old fellow's made of. Till, then, good-night.

[*Exeunt.*]

SCENE 3—*The same. A room in Wolford's house. Enter* WOLFORD.

Brandon is elected. The Half-breed scavengers are dead. That is consolation enough, but I mean more. What, Wolford, hast thou labored all thy life for this? Was it for this that thou wert born with genius? Was it for this that thou hast spent thy life in study? To be a dog following thy master, or a dull ass to pack him? To be the slave carrying one man to fame, but to return and fetch another? If so, thou hadst better take on the hide and hair of the beast thou art, and no longer wear the garb of man! No, Wolford, thou shalt no longer play the underling to any man. Now is thy time. That attribute which men lack most to make them great, is the ability to seize the opportunity, and make the time their own. But steady! Have thy wits about thee, for they are thy army. Train them well. Great Brandon, Walford made thee President! Behold! he will be generous. He will make thee Emperor. But thou dull, stupid, honest ox, whilst thou dost climb to glory Wolford will be thy rider. The rabble yells for thee. It only stares when Wolford passes; and therein lies thy usefulness; for, when the key's examined, all these shouts for Brandon are translated cries for Wolford. And those coin-handlers, stock-jobbers, grand larceny thieves, or, lest I might offend their graces, those money kings and railroad barons, shall all be my most chosen burglars to help pry open the hidden empire. They would make Brandon King that they might have their property secure. For the same reason they shall make Wolford King. And thy fine prancing fiery steeds, good Maxwell and McDonald, shall have their uses, too. What, ho! Hitch up the caravan! Fall in, asses; be yoked up, oxen; gallant horses; poor fools; put in a few locomotives! Now, Wolford, get thee in thy chariot; take up the reins. Go on, you motley team, and carry Wolford up the road to fame! This night the work shall be begun that ends in giving thee a throne. Quiet—here come my visitors.

Enter McDONALD, MAXWELL, RANDEMER, MINNARD, STARLOW, GEN. SHELBORN *and others.*

Good evening, gentlemen. It makes me happy to see you at my house after the stormy battle is so pleasantly ended.

McD. And we are no less glad to meet with one who, more than any other, brought about this great victory.

[RAN. *and* STAR. *move to one side of stage, while the rest remain conversing with* WOLFORD.]

Ran. (to Star.) Why not speak out your mind freely and plainly? I think I know the meaning that lies hidden beneath your half-spoken words.

Star. (to Ran.) Who made this country what it is? Who but we whose energy, brains and money, and money, I say, have dug canals, built railroads—

Ran. And made the desert to blossom like the rose.

Star. Why, but for us, it would have lain for centuries a howling wilderness.

Ran. And the Pacific and Atlantic been six months instead of only one short week apart.

Star. We pay all the taxes to support the Government, or nearly so.

Ran. Then why should not the Government be ours, since we made it and support it?

Star. And then, to think that after all we've done to build up this country, we are so repaid! Randemer, sometimes when I think of all I have done for me country, and then how she has repaid me, it almost makes these old eyes weep!

Ran. Repaid! Repaid! Why, damn me, sir, the only pay we ever get is to be howled at by every mob that gets together, and hounded down by a mean, contemptible press, that has to be subsidized and bought to silence!

Star. And then these legislatures! They are continually hampering us with laws, or threats of laws regulating our tariff, and interfering with us in a thousand ways, until we buy them up, body and soul. There's no end to their damned blackmailing schemes!

Ran. Starlow, it requires no very great foresight to see that at no distant day they will seek to confiscate our property—rob us of our hard-earned treasures.

Wol. (apart to Max.) Is Shelborn all right?

Max. It took all day to bring him over, but now he's the war est advocate of our cause. Do you notice Starlow and Randemer?

Wol. Yes; they are attracting the attention of everybody. I tell you, Maxwell, they are good royalists.

Star. I tell you, Randemer, I am tired of it.

Ran. And so am I. Why, this very year it cost us millions to elect our man. The country was made drunk with our coin.

Star. Why not end it now?

Ran You speak my thoughts. It must end some time, or we are ruined.

Star. A better time than this will never come. We are in power. At our head is a man of iron nerve, who never was defeated. A regular Bismarck.

Ran. His tremendous popular majority foreshadows his success in another direction.

Star. The time is ripe.

Wol. What did I hear you say, Starlow? The time is ripe? For what is the time ripe?

Star. 'M—what were we talking about, Randemer?

Ran. I think you must have misunderstood my friend, Senator. Were we not talking about corn being ripe?

Star. 'M—yes, so we were. The corn on the great plains. It is ready for shipment.

Wol. Bah! the corn was ripe two months ago. Gentlemen—my lords, shall I say? How finely that sounds. My Lord of California or the Duke of Erie, if you would prefer it.

Star. Senator, you joke in a hard way.

Wol. Come, sirs, the day was when to think or talk treason was treason, but treason is only treason now when it arises to the dignity of overt acts.

McD. Did I not hear some one speak of treason over here?

Max. Did I not hear some one say, my lord?

Min. If my ears deceived me not, I heard the name of Duke of Erie addressed to one who is or ofttimes has been called a baron.

Shel. And I hardly think the theme nor yet the titles fall unpleasantly upon the ears of any who heard.

Star. Little did I think when Randemer and I were talking that our thoughts found harmony with so many.

Wol. It is a little strange that each man coming here to-night should have brought a mind burdened with the same weighty thought.

Ran. Yet it seems true.

Wol. To speak it plainly—if there is one here present who does not want to see a change of government—in fact, to see the President elect President forever—or Emperor, if it please you—let him say nay.

Min. None speak. Why, if we all came here thinking the same thing, and only a chance gave utterance to our thoughts, who knows but millions in this great country may think as we do?

Wol. And thinking so will gladly act when a bold leader speaks to them.

Star. But hold you gentlemen, my lords, without a head a body is a useless thing. We are the trunks, Brandon the head of this great enterprise, and ere the body moves, the head must first consent.

Ran. Is there one here so bold as to approach him with this subject? Wolford, you are his friend, and, if I mistake not, close wrapped up with him. What say you?

Wol. Let me waylay your fears. Not thrice in all the history of the world has mortal man refused a proffered crown! Ambition is the motive power that moves the world. . To wear a crown or even a noble's garb, hundreds have placed their heads within the hangman's noose, or on the fatal block. But why does the President not come?

Shel. I should have told you, Wolford, that, when I left the General this evening, he said he would be here at ten. But to the point. How shall we carry our great enterprise to him who shall be Emperor?

Min. Let me suggest a way. This very night the close of the banquet I will propose a toast, "The future of our President-elect," and I will mark you (to Wol.) Senator—Senator yet a little while—to make response. And therein you shall speak gently, only refer to the less greater heads that wear golden crowns beset with diamonds, and rule the destinies of nations. I have no words like yours, Senators; you will arrange the style. Then speak how gracefully such a crown would rest upon America's most illustrious son. At this let each applaud, and all look straight at the great worrior, and, if I lie not, beneath those stoic features will be seen a blush of pleasure that would make pale the red cheeks of a new-made bride. The içe thus broken, let each man say his say.

Shel. The plan's a good one.

Wol. I would I had more time to make me ready in; but I will do my best. 'Tis but a moment now 'till ten. Let us receive the coming monarch in the banquet-room.

Ran. Caution our motto.

McD. That's a wise remark. [*Exeunt.*]

SCENE 4.—*The same. A banquet room. Seated around the table,* BRANDON, WOLFORD, McDONALD, MAXWELL, MINNARD, RANDEMER, STARLOW, SHELBORN *and others.*

Min. Before this joyous festival, in honor of our most distinguished friend, dissolves, I would propose a toast, nominating as I do so Senator Wolford as respondent. "The Future of our President-elect."

Wol. The subject is a great one, and on that account I should have known the toast before, that I might have made greater preparation to do the subject justice. Often set speeches are deceptive, being coined, as counterfeiters make base money, at dead of night, while the unprepared speech is the true outpouring of the soul, and so I speak on this occasion. [To Brandon]: Thy triumphal march from boyhood to the present, through battles that have shook the earth, through all degrees of honor which a devoted nation could confer upon thee, speaks like a thunder-blast from heaven, that the Great Ruler of the Universe has given thee special guidance. Of thy past I speak not, save as it is the mirror of thy future. If it has thus been heaven's will that thou shouldst grow each year in greatness, what power is there which saith to thee now, "Hold! Here must thou pause!" Could Nature have intended that in the rich luxuriance of thy manhood, thou shouldst stop, stand still, decay and rot? May not thy future have for thee a greater greatness than thy past? O, if my soul with a prophetic power were endowed, methinks that I could see a vision equalled alone by that which Moses saw upon the shores of Jordan! Not long ago I journeyed through the old monarchies of Europe, and I beheld in all their glory the rulers of those great countries. As I looked on them, clad in their stately uniforms, surrounded by their royal splendor, I could not help but draw comparisons between them and an American I knew—an honest, sober, unambitious citizen, but one of God's true noblemen, and each time I thought, how better far than they would he become those most majestic places. My mind dwelt upon the subject, and still I thought, if in my country, ever mortal man should wear a crown it should be Brandon. [Applause. Brandon attempts to rise, but sits down in confusion.] Another thing I noticed there: the hard-earned property of the rich was well protected, while those whom God made poor were happier in their poverty. If ought that I have said foreshadows the future of our President-elect, I shall be happy. This is my heart unbosomed. [Applause.]

Bra. Oh! my friends, ye know not—

McD. Nay, they are my thoughts, too.

Bra. Oh! friends—

Max. And mine.

Bra. Hear me.

All. And mine. (All rise.)

(*Curtain.*)

ACT II.

SCENE 1—*New York. A parlor in* MINNARD'S *house.*

Enter CATHERINE MINNARD.

I must not think! Yet, when the most I say I must not, then do I think the most. If I could only tear out memory from my brain! Oh, thou accursed attribute, that makes me live in a gallery of all my sins! Remembering kills me. O, God, why didst thou make us mortals as we are? Strike thou love from woman's heart, then will we all be good. Fain would my mind beg great excuses for my heart. Catherine, this trifling with thyself will never do. Out! thou stinging viper! Away from me! I have use for sterner qualities to-day than weak, meddling conscience. Clarence, thou shalt soon be here. O, wert thou born of woman, or did'st Venus with great Jupiter conceive thee. Gods! how I worship thee, Clarence! Great Nature made thee for me. Else, why this bursting heart? And why this mind, that thinks but of thee? And why this soul that would give heaven for thee? Why this great gravitation to thee, mighty as that which holds a planet to the sun? Wilt thou never come! (Goes to the window.) What demon drove me here to see my gentle, tender Leonora? O, now my weaker nature overcomes me! Shall I see her? Yes, once again, before my heart turns iron, and my blood to poison. Nora!

Nora. (From without.) Yes, mother.

Cath. Mother! How strangely she answers. She were wont to call me Mamma. 'Tis but a fancy of my armed imagination.

Enter NORA.

Dearest daughter! (Holds out her arms.)

Nora. (Embracing Catherine.) Did every daughter have a mother so good and pure and true as mine, how happy all this world would be!

Cath. Do you love me, Nora?

Nora. Do I love thee, mother? Why, how strangely you speak and act! How thy hand trembles! Art thou not well, mamma?

Cath. Wilt thou always love me, Nora?—always? always?

Nora. Dearest mamma, if thou couldst only look into my heart and see how much I love thee, thou wouldst never ask. What makes thee ask me, mamma?

Cath. I know you love me, darling; there—kiss me now.

Nora. But, mamma, I fear you are not happy. Will you not tell your Nora what it is?

Cath. 'Tis nothing, child. Art thou happy, Nora?—quite, quite happy?

Nora. Why do you ask such questions, mother?

Cath. Because, my darling, I thought of late you rather tried to avoid me. You seldom came to kiss me; and when I looked at you, your eyes so quickly sought some other resting-place. (Aside)—Perhaps it was my own dared not look straight!

Nora. Why, mother! (in confusion).

Cath. Nay, darling; hast thou seen some lover, tall and strong, with brown locks hanging o'er his noble forehead, and eyes that could look love itself? (Nora weeps.) (Aside.) Ah! now I think I have described my own Clarence. (Aloud.) Why, I should not have spoken so, my gentle child. Thy heart is far too tender. Forgive me. There, I meant nothing, dear. I know thou wilt never have a lover but thou wilt tell thy mamma first. Go, now, my child. (Kisses Nora.) [*Exit* NORA.

(Catherine falls on her knees.) O, if my miserable soul can but approach Thy throne, my prayer is, God of goodness, guide thou the feet of my darling child!

Enter WOLFORD.

Wol. What, Catherine, are you not well? You look so pale and your cheeks are tear-stained!

Cath. O, Clarence, when thou art from me I cannot help but grieve thy absence. Behold! these eyes have wept for thee; but now, since thou art come, they weep no more, unless it be for joy.

Wol. Some day this cloud, that now obscures our sun, shall melt away.

Cath. O, that that happy day should come ere long!

Wol. And so it shall, sweet Catherine.

Cath. Is it a crime that I should love thee? Nay, wait not for thy reason to answer; say no, quickly.

Wol. The suddenness of thy question startled me. Is it wrong for the warm sun to shine upon the cold earth, giving it life? Is it a crime for the gentle rain to keep the tree from dying? When thou shalt answer me yes, to these questions, then will I say thy love for me is wrong.

Cath. Dear Clarence, I thank thee for thy answer. I shall live upon it. Canst thou doubt my love?

Wol. Not though my life depended on it.

Cath. O would it did, that I might save it by it!

Wol. Sweet Catherine!

Cath. Hast thou a trust unlimited in me?

Wol. Aye, that I have, my love; but why these questions? Canst thou doubt me?

Cath. O, awful thought! Doubt thee? Doubt thee, Clarence? To doubt thee were to die; to die a thousand deaths upon each doubt. O, flee, unworthy thought! I asked thee these that I might ask thee one more question.

Wol. Let me but know thy question and thou shalt have my answer.

Cath. Then tell me, Clarence, what mighty matters bears upon thy mind?

Wol. Why, nothing save the ordinary affairs of life.

Cath. Nay; now you neither love nor trust me. The cares of life have long existed, but not so thy humor. In times gone by, in good society, thou wert an entertainer of the whole company; but now thou standest with brows drawn down, into a deep, black frown, and stare for long, long moments into the fire or still more empty space; and when disturbed by those who craved thy company, thou wert startled as a dreamer from his sleep, looked much annoyed and thanked them not for their kindly interruption.

Wol. Perhaps my inattentions to the graces of good breeding were caused by some momentous argument in course of preparation, lingering in my mind after the cares of the day should have been forgotten.

Cath. Have arguments become so all important lately?

Wol. I have thought much of thee.

Cath. But I have observed thy strange manners even when we were alone. Thy mind seemed fled its house and occupying some foreign castle, holding it a close prisoner. Oh, Clarence, put me not off with vain excuses. Trust me, oh, trust me! I will never prove thee false. Dost thou fear me? Has not my woman's heart convinced thee, that for Catherine there is but one in all this world? But trust me, and I will be as guarded of thy secret, as a lioness of her young. And thou shalt never ask my help but that my life—my very soul—shall be at thy command.

Wol. Oh, noblest woman that e'er took on a mortal garb; fit queen for any king that ever lived; my own true darling, Catherine, to thee will I confide my secret, trusting thee as I would a goddess.

Cath. My noble-hearted Clarence!

Wol. I will be brief. Thou knowest Brandon is President?

Cath. I know it should be thee instead of Brandon.

Wol. Yet is he not contented. His soul soars like the eagle.

Cath. What wants he else?

Wol. To be a king.

Cath. There is but one right royal head in all this land?

Wol. And we have formed a deep conspiracy to crown it.

Cath. Crown Brandon king? You?

Wol. Look not so startled, Catherine. That is our plan.

Cath. In all the over-bursting books of history there's not a traitor half so great as thou art. The meanest traitor therein mentioned is a patriot by thy side.

Wol. Why reproach me, Catherine?

Cath. That thou shouldst be so foul a traitor.

Wol. Hist, woman! Look how you speak! Oh, what a fool I was to tell you! Love makes men idiots; and, for women, empires have been thrown away, kingdoms scattered to the winds, and now another stately edifice fall from the same cause. From what thou say'st I would suppose thou wert a spy, set upon me by my enemies, to extort this secret from me, using my love and thy pretended love for me as mediums for the accomplishment of thy base ends; or else thou hast no conception of our mighty enterprise.

Cath. So do I like to hear thee speak, for now I know thou art not dead. Before I thought thou hadst turned a worm—a very grub. Still thou art a traitor—a traitor to thyself.

Wol. If there is any meaning in your words, I understand it not.

Cath. Dear Wolford, let me then inform thee. Thou takest up arms to make him King, who should be King thyself; therefore thou dost rebel against thyself, and thus thou art a traitor to thyself.

Wol. Your speech is still but little short of riddle.

Cath. Then let me solve it for thee. I may infer, from what you say, that there is a conspiracy on foot to make Brandon Emperor of this far-famed land?

Wol. Well?

Cath. And you are one of the conspirators?

Wol. Well?

Cath. To make Brandon Emperor; and you—you shall be his lieutenant; mayhap, if you are good you might be minister, or at least you will be my lord chamberlain and janitor of His Royal Majesty's private chambers!

Wol. Oh, Catherine, you ridicule our project.

Cath. Or, if those high positions be occupied by more fortunate courtiers for royal favor, you might, by begging it, be master of the hounds!

Wol. Tut, woman!

Cath. Or else, perhaps, be tutor to his children, and slapped in the face occasionally by a young prince.

Wol. If you continue, Catherine, I will swear you do not love me.

Cath. And if you continue, Clarence, I will swear I do not love thee—yea, more, that I hate, despise, detest thee!

Wol. What, woman! has it come to this?

Cath. So say I—has it come to this, that thou, great Wolford, upon whom Nature spent her choicest labors to form and robe and deck thee with all the god-like attributes of a sovereign, should play the underling to any mortal man? Oh, forgive me, Clarence, if mine enthusiasm has encroached upon my love; it was my love that made it do it. I would see thee Emperor—not Brandon; and so thou shalt be, unless worms catch eagles!

Wol. O, darling Catherine! O, noble Catherine! it should be I who, on my bended knees, begged thy forgiveness.

Cath. Nay—up; thy knees were never made to bend. Say thou shalt be the King; till then I never will forgive thee.

Wol. Then do I swear it. I shall be the king. O, Catherine, this hour hath taught me that thy arm is stronger and thy mind greater by far than Wolford's! Dost thou know the path that leads to this high honor? Canst thou tell me how I can be the King?

Cath. I am but a woman, Clarence, and fear me my advice has been already too profuse. But since you ask me, I will say, the same way that leads Brandon on to glory opens up for thee a crown.

Wol. Be a little plainer, Catherine. My brain is dull to-day.

Cath. In this conspiracy I see thou art the moving spirit. Thou art the camel that carries Brandon over the desert road to fame. Then overthrow him; become thyself the man; make him thy beast and seize the crown thyself.

Wol. If I had thy dauntless spirit, I think I could.

Cath. Then take it. I would die—give up my spirit if I could only greater thine.

Wol. O, noblest woman! If I am ever King thou shalt be Queen, or heaven and earth shall be o'erturned!

Cath. Alas! that cannot be. I have a husband and thou hast a wife.

Wol. Yes, so we have, and we can ne'er be happy while they live. They are great monuments in our road to happiness and glory. If they had more glory I would willingly give them both monuments.

Cath. What thought is this which runs like fire through my brain? What, Catherine! What! Oh, I am crazy! My mind is gone. Clarence, protect me from myself.

Wol. Calm thyself, Catherine. What were thy thoughts?

Cath. Methought I saw my husband's hated form lying beside me on our bed, a flood of moonlight through the window streaming o'er us. Methought I raised myself upon one arm and looking at those closed eyes said, *Closed be ye forever.* Then gently slipping from our couch, I took a long and double-edged dagger from out a drawer close by, then going back, leaned o'er that sleeping form and hissed: *Thou standest between me and my happiness; sleep thus forever.* And so, methought, I plunged the dagger to the hilt into his heart, then opened up the doors and called out murder! murder! Such thoughts, O Clarence, coursed like lightning through my crazy brain.

Wol. Be not affrightened, Catherine! Thy thoughts were strange; but while you saw such sights I had a kindred vision.

Cath. Hadst thou a vision too? O, strange occurrences! What saw you?

Wol. I saw at Wolford's home a woman that was called his wife, yet wife in name alone, grow sick and sicker every day with some affection of the heart. At last all hope was lost, of her recovery, and suddenly she died.

Cath. Ended thy vision there?

Wol. No. Next I saw two funeral courses passing with royal pomp the same day. The plumed hearse of one contained thy husband; the other held my wife.

Cath. And was that all?

Wol. O, next I saw a sight whose grandeur ne'er was equaled.

Cath. O, tell me quickly, Clarence!

Wol. I saw a royal, stately throne, in this great country. Upon it sat a king and queen, and all the nations of the earth paid homage to them.

Cath. Knew thou the king and queen?

Wol. As all passed by, I heard them shout: "Hail! Clarence, King! Hail! Catherine, Queen!"

Cath. For that these hands would reek in human blood.

Wol. These visions are prophetic. My part shall be done.

Cath. And mine!

SCENE 2—*Same. A room in* BRANDON'S *house.* BRANDON *seated, as if in deep study. Enter (unseen by* BRANDON), WOLFORD, MCDONALD *and* MAXWELL.

Wol. He is deep engaged in the subject, now. See! Now he looks upon it favorably; how he doubts; now he dreams of a second Napoleon. His moods are fickle yet not unfavorable. See how his feelings are depressed! We must infuse our spirits in him strong.

McD. Transplant thy own into him, Wolford. Look! He needs thy dauntless courage.

Max. Shall we not speak to him? I fear he might be angry should he discover us observing him in this condition.

Wol. Soft, now! Back to the door again, and all come in as if we had not been here. [They retire out of the door, then come in quickly.]

Wol. Good morning, General. We entered unannounced, your servant telling us you had left such orders.

Bra. Right, my friends. Good morning. You are always welcome, and need no announcement. Cards are for ladies, and their sisters, ladies'-men.

McD. Ah, General, I fear some gallant has superceded you in some quarter, that you should strike so hard at them this morning. Perhaps our beautiful and accomplished Mrs. Minnard failed to smile upon you last evening.

Max. If so, I suffered the same fate. The lady seems to save her smiles for my lord Wolford. How is it, Clarence?

Wol. Come, gentlemen, weightier matters should engross our time to-day than the questionable occupation of the discussion of a lady's favors. We bring good news this morning, General. Randemer, Minnard and Starlow have secured the support of every man they have approached. Of course, they have been discreet. We are backed by the finances of the nation. All the important railroads are ready to furnish us transportation for men and arms. The telegraph is at our service.

Max. Shelborn has made complete arrangements for taking possession of all the armories and forts.

Bra. O, gentlemen—friends—think me not lacking in courage; but there is something in it all I do not like.

Wol. What is it, General? It shall be righted.

Bra. No—there it is; it cannot be righted. It is the overturning of a government, established by our fathers, as a home for liberty, and the substitution of a monarchy.

Wol. Dear General, the history of the world informs us that democracies are only fitted for a people in their infancy. We have outgrown that boyish period. Babes are all equal when they are new born. When they grow up, some by a natural power become the rulers of the others. This is God's will, else were it not the case. Let us not try forestalling the wisdom of divinity. Thou wert born to rule, and 'tis rebellion 'gainst heaven to forsake thy mission.

Bra. Think you the people generally demand it?

McD. Let their past favors to thee answer. From all this nation there was but one man could be their President. Twice was it so before. When thus three times they have raised their voices for thee, wilt thou wait longer for the final call? Wouldst thou have them grasp thee by main force and hold thee on the throne?

Wol. If it wert thou alone who would be bettered by this change, I would speak slowly for thee. But, behold! thy country's good and thine own are one. What are we? A nation, a confederacy, a union—a something no man ever yet defined! A vast extent of territory, a huge mass of indefinable nothingness; two scores of petty sovereignties, pulling contrary to each other—a fruitful source for fierce intestine quarrels! What a farce, that being such we call ourselves great! Great in what? Nothing save our square miles. If thou wert Emperor, thou shouldst weld all these scraps, these broken masses, into a solid block, give to it shape, form, character; and then thy kingdom—O, shade my eyes from such a sight!

Max. Gods, what a sight! How pale and insignificant look all the monarchies of Europe by its side. To England—an island to the world. As Germany—a petty despotism to a God-ruled sovereignty. As Spain—a Liliputian to great Hercules. As Austria—a hand-organ to the music of the spheres. O, what a country thou shalt be the Emperor of!

McD. The arts and sciences, growing beneath thy fond paternal hand, shall make the dead of Greece and Rome grow envious.

Max. The industries, fostered by thy protecting care, shall furnish thy people's wants without depeudence upon other lands.

Wol. And if thy people, grown too soft by peace, should need infusion of the hard'ning qualities of war, or if thy martial spirit should seek for conquest, upon thy north lie the fair provinces of Canada, and on thy southern boundary is the rich but weak Mexican Republic, whose people—when thy greatness shall be known—shall long to have thee for their ruler too. And further southward the discordant states of Central and of South America but await thy coming, when the great continent, which Nature made but one, shall be beneath thy most imperial sway, and then the gods shall sigh and wonder that so great a man as thou wert ever born!

Bra. O, gentlemen—O, friends, forgive me if I leave you. My spirit is sore troubled, and my soul would with itself commune.

[*Exit* BRA.

McD. What think you, Wolford—will he resist the crown?

Max. Will he resist it?

Wol. Resist the crown! resist the crown! Maxwell! McDonald! why have ye lived so long, to ask me such a question? Can your bare eyes resist the dazzling splendor of the sun? If so, then Brandon can resist the crown. [*Exeunt.*

CURTAIN.

ACT III.

SCENE 1—*Washington. A park with a rustic seat. Night. Moonlight.*

Enter BRANDON.

Bra. O, mighty circumstances—O, weighty thoughts which bear so heavily upon me! Depression overcomes me; I am bowed down beneath a load too great for me to carry. Here let me rest my body, if my spirit will not. [*Sits down in seat in attitude of deep thought.*]

Enter ONEIROS *and* MORPHEUS *from behind* BRANDON. *They approach him noiselessly and wave their wands over his head.* BRANDON *gradually falls asleep. After he sleeps—*

Morpheus. Dream thou, sleeper, of thy coming empire.

Oneiros. Of thy future kingdom dream thee.

Morp. Call, Oneiros—call our helpers.

Onei. God of Dreamland, I obey thee.

[Oneiros retires to back of stage and, by waving his wand, causes the scenery to open, revealing a fairy land, and beckoning, through opening,

Enter IKELOS *and* PHOBETOR, *who approach* MORPHEUS, *and pay obeisance to him.*]

Morp. (to Ikelos). This sleeper would be an emperor; make thou his dreams appear realities.

Ikelos [performing over Brandon]. Obedient to the God of Dreams I, his assistant, breath my spirit through thee. Thus shall thy dreams to thee appear great realities.

Morp. (to Phobetor). To thee the powers the gods did give to make a sleeper's dreams alarming. Upon him put thy best effects.

Phobetor (performing over Brandon). Alarm I put into thy sleep; most startling be thy dreams.

Morp. Sweet Oneiros, will thou bring the goddesses of nightmares?

[Oneiros retires to rear of stage, and, by performing with his wand, causes the scenery to open, through which

Enter three Fatui.

Morp. Come, thou gods and goddesses of dreams, visions, fantasies and nightmares, let us circle round this sleeper, thus by our united efforts all our powers on him bestowing. [They circle round Brandon with fantastic motions.] Soft! Now he dreams. Let us, away, brothers and sisters.

[*Exeunt.*]

Bra. [rising, as if in a dream]. Yes, Wolford, thou art right. I must decide it now. But two days more e'er the inauguration. * * * Why, yes; I think thy arguments are sound. Good Clarence, I will confide in thee. I am sore, pulled, twisted and wrought-up to fever-heat by a fierce war that's waging in me. The armed hosts of patriotism and ambition are tearing my vitals out. * * * * Ha! Ha! How light a thing you make patriotism seem. * * * Well, so 'tis; 'tis a delusive occupation. To give all one's life for one's country and die a pauper! To have one's legs and arms shot off, and live upon a miser's pension! Or, if like me, escape these pains to suffer the stings, slurs and ingratitude of an ungrateful people. * * * Too true, too true. Who cares for all those countless millions who have laid down their lives for that vain thing we call a country? * * * * Why, now, you ask me who live in history: unless it is all a lie, they are those who have made their country's glory subservient to their own. * * * You are right, Wolford—to be a king is everything; to be a so-called patriot is nothing. I will be the King. I swear it! * * * * Yes, I think the people want me; I am almost certain of it. * * * Oh, certainly we may expect some trouble from the rabble; but I know how to deal with rabbles. Gatling-guns and grape-shot for rabbles.

Enter NAPOLEON I.

Nap. Yes, thou art right. Gattling guns and grape-shot for rabbles.

Bra. Who speaks? What! Who is this with such close likeness to the great dead Emperor of France?

Nap. The immortality of the first Napoleon greets the coming Emperor of America!

Bra. The first Napoleon! The coming Emperor of America! What trick is this that so deceives my eye and ear? My heart would leave me, yet my blood stands frozen in my veins! O, speak —whence came thou? What wilt thou? O, do relieve my spell!

Nap. Fear not. Let thy strong limbs resume their uses, and thy heart beat moderate. I came not here to harm thee. If thou wouldst know from whence I came, I can but point thee to the past, and say: *from whence the millions of this earth have gone!*

Bra. Then art thou in reality the great Napoleon—the spirit in which France lived—the conqueror of the world—the banished Emperor?

Nap. Of whom thou speakest I am the immortal part, made visible to thee.

Bra. O, most transcendent genius of this earth, for what cause didst thou leave that unknown world to thus appear before a mortal man in human guise?

Nap. To tell thee that thou shalt be an emperor.

Bra. An emperor?

Nap. Aye; and thy children and their children, emperors.

Bra. O, great Past Majesty!

Nap. Thou shalt be Emperor of America. But ere thou dost join me in that other world, as an immortal king, the limits of the country over which thou shalt the ruler be, shall be the poles of earth.

Enter ALEXANDER THE GREAT.

Bra. O, wondrous night! What being art thou, who doth wear the looks of man and gods combined? Art thou of earth, or dost thou to that unknown realm belong?

Alex. Full two and twenty hundred years ago, like thee I was a mortal man, and then this earth I made my home.

Bra. Durst I to ask thee whom then thou wert, or would it be bold impudence to thus accost thee?

Nap. For thy sake will I answer, lest, should the information come from yonder source, thou'dst die of sheer amazement. Great Alexander, son of the Macedonian King, attends thee!

Bra. Oh, that my tongue had speech!

Alex. Nay, calm thyself. To greet thee, father of a race of kings, I left that far-off land.

Enter CÆSAR.

Bra. No man who ever lived upon this earth, save one, bore that great face, and he was Julius Cæsar.

Cæs. Whether my life deserved the rich encomium of your speech I will not say, but thou hast rightly called my name.

Bra. Immortal Cæsar, greatest of all the earth, humbly I bow before thee, yielding obedience to thee. Oh, wilt thou tell me, humble mortal that I am, why thou mad'st vacant thy great throne in space to dazzle thus my eyes?

Cæs. With these, my compeers of that other world, I came to hail thee King.

Enter FREDERIC THE GREAT.

Bra. And is this more departed, yet immortal royalty!

N. A. and C. Hail Frederic, great King of Prussia!

Fred. From my throne in yon bright firmament, to this, my former habitation, I came to see the crowned Emperor of America.

Bra. To see me crowned?

Fred. Aye, and to help in thy great coronation.

Enter CATHERINE II. *and* PETER THE GREAT.

N. A. C. and F. Hail, Catherine and Peter, great Empress and Czar of Russia.

Bra. Before that awful pair I bow in solemn awe. Honoring the earth with thy great presence I would welcome thee, save that thy right on this terrestial sphere is first o'er mine. As 'tis, I hail thee, greatest ruler that ever took the form of woman, and hail thee, noble Czar.

C. and P. And hail we to the coming monarch of the world.

Alex. Now, from our realm, comes the great Pharaoh of Egypt.

Enter an EGYPTIAN KING.

Cæs. And now, sweet Cleopatra, daughter of the Nile.

Enter CLEOPATRA.

Nep. My own example, Louis XIV., of France.

Enter LOUIS XIV.

Cæs. Great Hannibal, the Carthagenian general.

Enter HANNIBAL.

Bra. O, majesty! O, majesty! O, what a realm of kings and emperors, philosophers and statesmen, warriors and great heroes came ye from!

Nap. All the immortal greatness of the earth is there!

Bra. Blind not my eyes with more, lest that I take my life to see it all!

Cæs. Since we have come to place upon thy head the crown imperial of thy future state, what name wilt thou assume by which thy followers and all time shall know thee?

Bra. Mighty Cæsar, wilt thou christen me?

Cæs. Since so it is thy will, I will. From this time on, through all eternity, thou shalt be called Ulysses First, Emperor of America.

Nap. Come, now, ye lesser and attendant gods, bring forth the golden throne.

Enter a number of Nymphs, who, by waving their wands at rear of stage, cause the scenery to part, revealing a throne, which, in obedience to their movements, is by invisible hands pushed forward, when the scenery is again closed.

Nap. (to Nymphs.) Bring forth the royal robes. (*The Nymphs produce them.*)

Nap. Enrobe His Majesty for his coronation. (*The Nymphs enrobe Brandon.*)

Alex. Ascend thy throne, thou coming monarch. Attend! (*Brandon ascends the throne.*)

Cæs. Bring forth the diamond crown which from the other world we brought. (*The Nymphs bring the crown and give it to Cæsar.*)

Enter MERCURY.

Cæs. Swift-running Mercury, herald of the gods, hast thou message for us?

Mercury. From great Jupiter on high come I to Your Majesty.

Certain of the gods he sends to this coronation, and sweet goddesses attend on the great Ulysses.

Cæs. If it so please the gods and goddesses to attend the coronation of Ulysses as their herald, bid them enter.

Mercury retires to rear of stage, and with his caduceus or staff causes the scenery to open.

Mer. From thy throne on high, great Mars, come, thou thund'ring god of wars!

Thunder and lightning. Mars is seen as if coming out of clouds, and enters through rear of stage.

Enter MARS.

Mars. (Before the throne.) Great Ulysses, Emperor to be, God of War good greeting giveth thee. Full many a battle with earth's rulers thou shalt wage, and thrones shall crumble, kingdoms disappear, empires dissolve and nations fall before thy all victorious arms. Defeat shall never know thee, for thou shalt have the guidance of the gods.

Mer. (Opening scenery as before.) From out the ocean's pearly depth old Neptune cometh to the coronation.

[NEPTUNE *appears as if rising from the ocean and comes in at rear of stage and before throne.*]

Nep. Upon the seas thy nation once was great. Forsaken is old Neptune by it now. So does the God of Ocean leave it and upon thee bestow his blessings. When thou art Emperor thou shalt have a navy under whose weight the waters of the deep shall groan; not all the powers of the earth shall cope with it, for it shall be beneath the care of Neptune.

Mer. The Goddesses of Wisdom, Love and Justice pay attendance on Ulysses.

Cæs. Let them enter.

[*Enter* MINERVA, VENUS *and* THEMIS. *All come before the throne.*]

Min. Since thou shalt be the greatest ruler on this earth, 'twere well that thou shouldst have the greatest quality of such a king. Therefore know thee that it is wisdom. Greater in government is it than ships of war or belching cannon, or armed hosts, or money-bursting treasury. And thus as a free gift her goddess giveth it thee supreme.

Venus. The oldest monarch in this world is love. He hath more subjects and more riches than any other, for all mankind, yea even the very beasts do pay him tribute. His fields are boundless and his hidden treasures would make a universe of solid gold. If thou wouldst be so great an emperor, let all thy acts be filled to overflowing with my spirit. Venus doth bless thee, great Ulysses.

Themis. No quality—not even love—becomes so well a mighty ruler as doth cold and even-handed justice. Thou canst make no mistake if thou wilt take justice for thy guide. Her goddess, rivaling in her gifts to thee, wisdom and love, bestows her richest blessings on thee.

Mer. The fair goddesses of Peace and Home would enter

[*Enter, in same way as others,* EIRENE *and* HESTIA.]

Cæs. Gentle goddesses, came ye to give to great Ulysses your blessings?

Eirene and Hestia. Most mighty Cæsar, so we came.

[*They go before the throne.*]

Eirene. Think not I would upon the proper sphere of Mars encroach, nor yet make small the qualities of necessary war. Yet know thee, mighty monarch that thou shalt be, that in the arts of peace, not war, must lie thy real greatness. Eirene gives thee blessings.

Hestia. Hail, Sovereign Majesty, and know thee, that if thou wilt have thy kingdom rival Jove's, thou must teach thy people to have homes, for every one that has a home is a sovereign in himself, and thus shalt thy dominion be composed of sovereigns, and thou shalt be a king of kings.

Mer. Fame and Fortune would address thee.

Enter FORTUNA *and* FAMA.

Fortuna. All good fortune from my hand does come. All good fortune give I thee.

Fama. O'er this earth thy fame shall fly, to the world's remotest ends.

Mer. (coming before the throne). By their herald, Mercury, sends to thee, great Jupiter, and all the other gods their richest blessings. (To Cæsar.) Let the coronation now proceed.

Cæs. By the great counsel of immortal kings in our great realm, beyond the confines of the earth, it was decreed that Cæsar should place upon thy head the diamond crown, which thou shalt wear when thou art crowned by mortal man. Now, by the powers in me vested, I crown thee Ulysses First, Emperor of America [raises the crown to put it on Brandon's head.]

Enter WASHINGTON.

Wash. Stop thy accursed ceremonies, or the great King of kings will curse thee twice. Down, ye damned monsters of iniquity, ye fell traitors to humanity! Dyed are your hands and smeared your bodies o'er with the blood of all your countries. Would you increase the tyrants of this world by one? would you stir up a stormy revolution in this happy land, glut it with blood, kill off its sons? I'll send you back to your damned holes in hell, for you are on a mission from the devil. Back to your world of myths, delusive gods and goddesses. (To Brandon.) Oh, thou beastly glutton! Art thou not satisfied with all the honors of this free people? Must thou enslave thy countrymen to bring thee glory? No human head shall ever wear a crown in this free land. Give me that tyrant's headgear (snatches it from Cæsar). So as I cast this cursed thing upon the ground, shall thy head fall if thou dost ever try to play the tyrant in this country; crouch down, ye despots; I am your enemy. Think ye I fear your all-impotent rage? No, no! Nor shall my country. Preserve, oh, God, this people from the hands of tyrants and of kings.

[*Curtain.*]

ACT IV.

SCENE 1—*New York. A street.*

Enter WOLFORD.

Wol. Life is one long series of speculations, and the world's a huge stockboard. We are all either buyers or sellers—bulls or bears. All the propositions of life end in how many, how much, what amount, and their kindred. Every thing's for sale or exchange. Take, for instance, your honest politician and your dear people. One has an office to dispose of, and the other wants it. One says, How many inducements can you offer for it? the other answers, Behold! here's my honesty, or my sack, or my brains, or my long-nosed scheming, or my short-nosed fighting, or my honest trickery, and so on *ad infinitum*, till all your qualities of a politician are exhausted. The highest bidder takes the office. So with your lawyer, your doctor, your preacher, your merchant, your lover, your everybody. To-morrow a throne is to be disposed of. I am a bidder. As I am about to enter upon the largest series of transactions of my life, 'twere well I figure a little on my prospective profits and losses. I lose a wife—that's certain. Sweet spirit, take thy flight to heaven; my loss is thy gain. If I had lost thee long ago I had not died from grief. Next, I lose a friend, by name Wallace Minnard. What moots it, Clarence, that thou shouldst lose a friend? The world is full of them, and thou may'st have them for the picking. What! who said thy conscience? Well, 'tis a good riddance! But I have lost thee many times, and, like a worthless cur, thou dost come sneaking home again. If thou hadst been of any worth, some thief would have stolen thee long ago. Some day I'll murder thee outright, and then thou wilt follow me no longer. Now to my gains—for, after all, I like that side the best. I gain a wife; yes, I lose Miriam and I gain Catherine. 'Tis a good exchange. If I lose my dear friend Minnard, I gain his fortune, which, falling to his wife, shall reach me by the law—of gravitation. And it is said Minnard has stolen millions. I cry him, Stop, thief! deliver to an honest man! But these transactions employ only the little, mean and insignificant broker in me. They involve not my greater nature, but, like side-shows, are things to be looked into while we are where they are. A throne! a throne! an empire of fifty millions! Ye gods, the attempt to get it is worth a thousand deaths! Ah! here comes Catherine. If I had let the fair sex be, methinks I would have been a greater and a better man.

Enter CATHERINE MINNARD.

My dearest Catherine, the time speeds quickly when I hail thee as a queen.

Cath. To-night great deeds are done; to-morrow greater. Then must the iron bands of patience hold us for a little while, till public sentiment is satisfied, and after that—love! glory! fame!

Wol. Truly, Catherine; truly. If thou couldst have but one, which wouldst thou choose, love, glory or fame?

Cath. 'Tis for thy love that I do all. The others are thy own, and only mine as they are thine.

Wol. Most incomparable woman! But does thy courage ever fail thee?—art thou strong in thy determination?

Cath. Clarence, I see a star that is my guide. O, what a brilliant star! It never sets, but in its fixture shines through day and night, paling both sun and moon. 'Tis to that star that I am going, Clarence. Between that heavenly body and myself are raging torrents, deep gorges, high mountains and great oceans. All these must I pass, but I falter not. To one in this life, who has a set determination, nothing is impossible. Need I tell thee, Clarence, thou art my star?

Wol. Noble woman! With thee a man could be a king, face every obstacle, beat down conspiracies, wage war, and fix his throne as high as Jove. But we must not tarry here, lest gross suspicion fix his eye upon us.

Cath. Shall I not see thee once again before to-morrow? No one can tell what Fate—that awful word!—to-morrow may have stored up for us. Just once more, Clarence.

Wol. Yes; when the moon rises to-night, meet me in your garden by the great oak tree. 'Till then, adieu, brave spirit.

[*Exit* WOLFORD.

Cath. Why should I go? 'Tis much against my better judgment. There is a quality in human nature past finding out, that leads us on to risky places. But I must know whether she suspects me. Yes, to his wife—thither will I go. His wife! If she were not beneath contempt I would despise her. As 'tis, I almost pity her. We used to be great friends, but I have grown so great a coward of late, I have not dared to see her. Clarence says she is broken-hearted. I will go to her with a face so full of sympathy that even Satan might be deceived. Then will she the better be prepared to meet her fate, and I shall know if she attributes her lost sovereignty to me. [*Exit.*

SCENE 2.—*A room in Wolford's House. Miriam Wolford seated.*

Miriam. Oh, me! ah, me! and here I sit all day and sigh. Oh, me! Miriam, once thou hadst beauty, it is gone; once thou hadst spirit and ambition, but they are gone. Thou art but the dead, useless skeleton of thy once self. Yet I am his wife. At least I bear his name, and I have borne him children. Alas! I bear his name and am the mother of his children; nothing more. And he so great, so grand! Why, all the world fawns on him. I blame them not, if they all love him. God knows how I do. - And yet he is so cold to me. Have I lost all those charms with which I won him? Has my poor body grown so worthless that his warm blood congeals at sight of it? O, awful thought! No, no, not that; O, my poor wasted body! Yet 'tis so, and while he seeks his pleasures from his home, I must stay here tormented by a thousand demons. Oh, God! thou only knowest the sufferings of many a devoted wife and mother.

Enter servant, with card.

Servant. Madam: pardon me, madam.

Mir. I care to see no one to-day, Mary. Say I am sick. [Reads card.] Catherine Minnard—my old friend. Stay a moment, Mary. Let me think. She always was so kind. O, how I need some consolation! She waits upon the sick—no one so sick as I. She ministers to the poor—the poorest beggar is a millionaire by me. Surely she must have a heart that beats in unison with mine. Yes, I will receive her, if only that I may draw some sympathy from her presence. Mary, you may show Mrs. Minnard in.

Enter CATHERINE.

Cath. (aside). How my heart beats. I am full of misgivings; yet I must be cool. (Aloud.) Oh, Miriam! how glad I am to see you.

Mir. My dear old friend, I had almost thought you had forgotten me, it has been so long since you came to see me.

Cath. Think not it was because I did not want to see you, dearest Miriam. I have so longed to, but I have been so much engaged.

Mir. I know, dear; your time is all taken up in deeds of charity.

Cath. Why, Miriam, how pale you look. Have you not been ill? (Aside.) Why did I ask that question, to receive some answer that I do not want.

Mir. No, dear, not sick; I am as well as usual, I think.

Cath. I fear that you deceive me, dear heart, for I would have thought you were just recovering from some serious illness. (Aside.) Asking it again; how foolish I am.

Mir. Do I look so very bad?

Cath. You have been crying, Miriam. Is there not some trouble you are having you can tell me and with you let me sympathize? (Miriam bursts out crying.) (Aside.) O, worse than idiot head to put itself beneath the hangman's noose, and yet I cannot help it.

Mir. The kindness of your heart appeals to mine, and tells me you will help me bear my sorrow.

Cath. (Aside.) Did ever one so long and yet so dread to hear a story. But I must know if she know anything. (Aloud.) Dearest Miriam, pour thy sorrow in my ear, and if a woman's heart can help thee, then shall mine be thy willing servant.

Mir. Dear, kind Catherine, thou knowest that I have a husband.

Cath. Yes, Miriam.

Mir. And yet I have no husband.

Cath. Thou hast a husband and yet thou hast no husband. I fear I do not understand. (Aside.) Alas! I know her meaning far too well.

Mir. Fifteen years ago to-day Clarence and I were married. I had a husband then.

Cath. (Aside.) There is a hidden meaning in her words I do not like. (Aloud.) And is not he your husband still?

Mir. No; he that was my husband is so no more. He's dead.

Cath. What, dead? Did you say dead? Your husband dead? Oh, Miriam, that cannot be. (Aside.) Why, I left him not an hour ago. What does she mean?

Mir. Ah! Catherine, I knew that in a heart so warm as your's I would find sympathy.

Cath. Yes, if your husband's dead you have my whole heart's sympathy. It bleeds as your's bleeds, Miriam.

Mir. I say he's dead and yet he lives.

Cath. He's dead and yet alive? O, make your meaning clear.

Mir. 'Tis this, dear Catherine. Clarence is dead to me, his wife, and yet he lives for others.

Cath. Are you quite sure of what you say? Mayhaps you accuse your husband wrongly. Will you tell me what proofs you have?

Mir. Oh! evidence that to a woman's heart is too conclusive. He used to say, "I love you, Miriam," or "my own dear one," and cover me up beneath a load of such endearing phrases. But he says such things no more. And when, in times gone by, as was his custom in the morning, he quit our home to go about his usual avocations, he'd put his arm about me, and taking me thus to the door, fold me in his strong embrace and rain down kisses on my thirsty lips till I was flooded with his love. Then, coming home at evening, bring rich bouquets of flowers and other little love-tokens which his quick eye perceived I liked; and, supper over, would stay through the evening with me, or take me to places of amusement, to return home thence, to that fondest place, where, resting on his arm, I drowned in the oblivion of sweetest slumber. Alas! he does these things no more, but is sealed up, in cold, arctic apathy and inattention. 'Tis this that hollowed out my cheeks, made these ridges and furrows in my flesh, and sistered me to death.

Cath. But still, may it not be that these inattentions are but those ordinary ones which grow up between man and wife when years have dulled the ardor of their first affection? You know, Miriam, our husbands are not always what they were upon our wedding days, when they crusted us deep over with the honey of their love.

Mir. I might think so, were Clarence but an ordinary man, whose affection oozed out as he aged. But in him every nerve is a battery of love, and every artery flows full of blood charged with rich affection. No, Catherine, he gives that love that should belong to me unto another.

Cath. And know you who that other is?

Mir. No.

Cath. Have you no idea?

Mir. No, nor do I care. She who robs me of my husband is a harlot, whether she lives within a marble palace and is bedecked with diamonds, or in the gutter by the open advertisement of her unchastity. Oh, dear, kind soul, my tale of woe has much affected you.

Cath. Yes, dear, it has quite overcome me. You have all my sympathy. Oh, how I grieve to find you in such trouble. Be assured that if it rests in my power to help you in any way I shall do so. And now, dear Miriam, good-bye. Let not this deep affliction keep us from being friends, but rather let me help you bear it.

Mir. Oh, Catherine dear, you little know how much better I feel since I have found one kind heart in which to pour my sorrow.
[*Exit* CATHERINE.]
It is now Clarence's time for coming home. Home, did I say? Oh, what a meaning for that sweet word is this! Clarence, if thou would'st only show me just a little kindness! Somehow I feel a change is coming. It must be for the better. It can be no worse.

Enter WOLFORD *with a bouquet.*

Wol. My dear, I bought you a bouquet as I was coming home.

Mir. Oh, Clarence!

Wol. I thought you would like it; they are your favorite flowers.

Mir. Like it, Clarence? I worship it as I do the giver.

Wol. Oh, darling, if I have seemed of late to grow cold and neglectful of my love, vote it not that my love's grown cold, but rather that the affairs of state have weighed heavily upon my mind.

Mir. You are my own true Clarence. I knew there must be something great to keep my love so housed up in himself. Oh, happy day!

Wol. Yes, Miriam, this is a happy day, for you and I and millions. I will tell you, but you must not breathe it——

Mir. Not for the world.

Wol. That great conspiracies have been stalking o'er this land, seeking to overthrow the government, and it has required the promptest and most decisive action to thwart them.

Mir. And you have been among the first—yea, the very first—to dare everything for your country's sake!

Wol. But now it is all ended, and we shall be so happy.

Mir. And you will always be to me just as you used to be. Why, Clarence, what is this you have in your pocket? May I take it out?

Wol. Why, certainly, dear. I had forgotten all about it. It is an orange of a very peculiar kind, from South America. Will you eat it?

Mir. O, thank you, Clarence. (Peeling it.) Clarence, did you get it for me?

Wol. Yes, darling.

Mir. (Eating.) Why, what a peculiar tasting orange it is. It's so very sweet.

Wol. Therein lies its peculiar excellence. (Aside.) Some poisons are very sweet.

Mir. Clarence, there won't be any more conspiracies that will keep us separated, will there?

Wol. I hope not, Miriam.

Mir. And we will always be together. I am so happy. Do you know how much I love you?

Wol. How much?

Mir. More than all the world—more than my life. Tell me that you love me, Clarence.

Wol. My first, my only love, thou knowest that my love for thee is boundless.

Mir. Oh! Clarence, what a peculiar feeling I have about my heart. It seems to flutter for an instant and then almost stop.

Wol. What can it be, I wonder?

Mir. There, I am better now. I think it was the thought that my dear Clarence had come back to me. (Struggles.)

Wol. (Aside.) Oh! have I lost all feeling? Am I iron?

Mir. What did you say, Clarence? O, my heart! I cannot breathe! (Dies.)

Wol. Miriam, thou art dead, and my mind hangs on a pivot, knowing not whether to be glad or sorry. Thou wert a good wife, as good wives go in this bad world, and I rather think thy proper sphere was heaven. For all thy goodness to me I was thy debtor; now I have paid thee with an angel's robe. I cannot mourn thee now as thou deservest, for other thoughts engross me. In due course of time thy body will be found, where thou didst suddenly die of heart disease; then will I follow thee, all muffled up in sorrow, to thy grave. Farewell. I must to Catherine now.

SCENE 3—*A garden. The moon just rising.*

Enter LEONORA MINNARD *with a bible and a vial.*

Nora. O, heart—O, heart of me! O, Nora, Nora, Nora! far too young thou didst find out thou hadst a heart. Ah, this awakening! O, saddest hour, when maidens wake from the sweet sleep of their virginity, to find it ravished from them! What curse did bring this on me? He was so good, so noble and so kind; one would have thought that heaven had been his teacher. No flower was ever half so sweet as those honey words with which he stole my soul. Oh! I can hear them now as they creep through my nerves, holding me charmed before him. Life for me is ended. My body, sapped of its honor, is a worthless thing—fit food for worms. (*Kneels, holding the book up before her.*) Oh, Holy Virgin, pure mother of our blessed Savior! wilt thou give intercession for my poor soul?

Enter CATHERINE, *not perceiving* NORA.

Cath. Softly! This is the hour I was to meet him here.

Nora. (not perceiving Catherine.) Dear, sweet, pure mamma, I shall never see thee more!

Cath. What! Nora here?

Nora. Oh, papa—gentle, loving papa! God in heaven, wilt Thou be their guide? Give them strong hearts to bear this awful sorrow; they shall never know their darling's shame. (*Lifts bottle and takes poison.*)

Cath. O, Nora, Nora! my child, my child! (*Catches bottle.*)

Nora. Mother!

Cath. Dearest child—my only child—what awful sorrow is it makes thee do this woeful act?

Nora. Oh, mamma, dare I approach thy holy person ere I die? Can I call thee mother still? I can never look thee in the face.

Cath. God in heaven, spare me! oh, strike me dumb, that I may never hear this! oh, pluck out my eyes, that I may never see this!

Nora. Do not reproach me, mother; I pray thee, by all the love thou once didst bear poor Nora, give me one little drop of pity.

Cath. If I had only died before this day! Thou great Eternal Power, I do await Thy stroke.

Nora. Oh, mother! let me lay my head upon thy breast and die.

Cath. Wilt not Thou kill me? cannot I die? how I do pray for death!

Nora. Say thou dost forgive me; then I can die.

Cath. What, Nora! Is my grief so great I cannot think of thee? Oh! my poor child! My little lamb!

Nora. Can you forgive me, mother? How he loved me! 'Twas all in love I yielded. Oh, Clarence, for thy love do I forgive thee!

Cath. (Throwing Nora from her.) What name is that that tears my hearing from me? Oh! beast! This is completed retribution. Sealed be my woman's heart forever! Out, pity! Out, remorse! Out, conscience! Out, everything! Give room for vengeance! Vengeance, fill up my soul! Where is that dagger that was brought to murder Wallace? (Producing it.) Thou shalt perform a holier office now.

Enter WOLFORD, *not perceiving* NORA.

Wol. My sweetest Catherine, thou art waiting for me?

Cath. Yes, I am waiting for thee, traitor!

Wol. Thou art a noble actress, Catherine. With what great sternness thou didst pronounce me traitor, my pretty coadjutrix.

Cath. Back, villain! Wouldst thou defile me more with thy accursed, tainted touch?

Wol. The greatest patriot could not have said it better. Thou art a queen by nature.

Cath. See'st thou this dagger? It was bought to murder Wallace!

Wol. Why, 'tis a pretty weapon, and will still his heart most beautifully.

Cath. It shall still thine, if one thou hast, thou thrice-accursed traitor!

Wol. (Aside.) It seems to me there is something more than acting here. (Aloud.) If I a traitor am, thou art my accessory, my partner, as thou shalt be my queen.

Cath. Was not thy gourmand heart satisfied when thou betrayed thy country and thy friends?

Wol. Not till I am a king and thou a queen.

Cath. Was't not enough that thou should'st steal my wifely honor!

Wol. What, madam! You carry your play too far! Enough! Enough! 'Twas not for this I came here.

Cath. Oh! thou incestuous devil! Look yonder, and prepare to die! (Points with her dagger to Nora.) O that I knew some art by which I could kill thee perpetually! Crouch, coward! Crouch before thy devilish work!

Wol. O, spare me, Catherine, for my love to you!

Cath. Thy love that was so great that thou didst blind and make me deaf to all my duty! Thy love that was so great that thou didst steal my virtue! Thy love that was so monstrous that thou didst rob me of my richest treasure! O monstrous love! For thy great love for Catherine thou shalt die. She'll let thy blood out. Yet stay. If I kill thee, coward that thou art, thy suffering shall be but momentary. No! Thou shalt live to die a million times each day, if in thy traitorous heart remorse holds any place. 'Tis I shall die, and thou my murderer and that sweet babe's. And every hour thou livest thy accursed vision shall see before it Catherine and Nora. Out from my sight, thou viper. I could not die with thy false eyes upon me.

[*Exit* WOLFORD.

Oh! my sweet darling, thy mother's sins descended on thee. I could weep my very soul out, if that would give thee back thy virgin purity. Thy soul has gone to thy Redeemer.

Nora. Mamma!

Cath. Not dead! Oh! that thou hadst not seen thy mother's face again.

Nora. Dear mamma, give me thy forgiveness e'er I die.

Cath. Alas! Thou hast it, Nora. 'Tis I should ask thee thy forgiveness. Thou knowest not thy mother's shame.

Enter MINNARD, *clothed in the Court dress of a nobleman.*

Min. To be a nobleman! My wealth and my life's work are worthy of it. To what high station have I not attained. Yet on to-morrow shall all things be completed. Why should I not try on my dress and wear my sword in this my garden, unperceived by any one. [Sees Catherine, who has turned toward him on her knees, as if in a trance.] Catherine here! My wife, and on her knees. What means this strange proceeding?

Cath. Could not high heaven have spared to my burning soul this last exhibit?

Min. Why art thou in this plight; thy eyes all blood-shot and thy face with such strange marks upon it? Up, wife? Knowest thou that on to-morrow thou shalt be a duchess?

Cath. To-night my vilest soul shall be in hell.

Min. Thou art gone mad! Some demon possesses thee.

Cath. Nay; touch me not, lest thou too be defiled.

Min. Defiled? Do my ears hear rightly, or am I in a dream?

Cath. O, would to God thou wert!

Min. Catherine, throw off this deep demeanor. Have I wronged thee, that thou shouldst so treat me?

Cath. Yes, past all forgiveness, that thou shouldst have one gentle pitying look for me.

Min. Forgive me, darling wife, if I have e'er done aught but love thee. For ever since I took thee as my wife, my pledge to honor thee has ne'er been broken.

Cath. Oh! pity; have some pity, else will my soul be damned before I die.

Min. Poor dear, some complaint to which thy sex is wedded has o'erthrown thy reason. Come, let me take thee in these arms that ever will protect thee from all harm, and when thy body has from the all-refreshing night drawn rest, the morning will return to thee thy sound strength. (Seeing Nora.) What, Nora! and prostrate on the earth! What foul crime is this that has, with one fell blow, bereft my wife of reason and stricken my gentle daughter like a dull cold corpse upon the ground? Speak! Unloose thy tongue, or, by the gods, I will disown thee as my wife!

Cath. Alas! I know not how to speak; I only know I am the vilest mortal on this earth. Oh! thou who wert my husband, to ask thee to forgive me were to outrage heaven. Unsheath thy sword and kill me, who has brought dishonor on thee.

Min. A foul suspicion creeps into my unwilling mind. Catherine, hast thou betrayed thy marriage vows?

Cath. Oh, kill me, Wallace, kill me!

Min. Not till thy heart ungorges it foul secret.

Cath. 'Twas the dazzling genius of thy false friend that blinded me to all my duty. Think not that I attempt excuses. False traitor, Wolford, he it was who robbed thee of thy wife, and, uncontented still, sacked the pure virtue of thy only child. Here lies she dead by her own hand, and so I end my worthless life. [Stabs herself.]

Min. Stand I so? Can I do naught but feast my eyes upon destruction? Where is thy manhood, Minnard? Unsheath thy sword, that never yet knew human blood, nor scabbard it again till with the blood of doubly-false Wolford it is covered. [*Exit* MINNARD.

Enter WOLFORD.

Wol. She forbade me see her die, but placed no interdiction on a view of lifeless flesh. Now I can look upon thee, dumb, cold, spiritless body, and my abhorred form be seen not by thee. This is the richest desolation that I ever saw. Why, I could see the grave-yards of the world plowed up, and dead men piled as high as heaven; could look upon a field of battle strewn with dead, or—still more awful—dying; could gaze upon the suffering of hell: and my gross appetite for crime be only whetted. But this dire scene, thwarting my inclination, somewhat troubles me. That little drop of pity which long years of sin has covered over with a deep, hard, heavy coating, bursts its bounds, and my boyish spirit like a flood comes over me. Oh! now I wish you were not dead, and that my life had been less badly spent. Catherine, I know now that I loved thee. Thou hadst a great nature that close fitted mine. Thy being was a strange commingling of strength and weakness. Thy greatest quality was love. It led thee on to deeds of charity and greatest kindness, and it led thee to thy doom. (*Looking at Nora.*) If I could know remorse, I think that it would overwhelm me when I look on yonder sight. But such a feeling is beyond my nature. If my repentance could put life into thy pretty, childish form, I would repent—aye, so I do, though 'tis a worthless task.

Enter Ghost of woman with child in her arms.

To longer look upon thee would break my manhood down and unprepare me for my other work. To-morrow the crown is to be played for, and I must away. (*Turns to go and is confronted by the ghost.*) What form from hell is this?

Ghost. Thou once didst know me, traitor.

Wol. Thou liest. All knowledge of thee I disclaim.

Ghost. Why, Wolford, now thou speakest like one who would

throw off the memory of some past crime. Disclaim! 'Tis a wise course, though any fool might take it. Disclaim! Say thou hast forgot. Damn thy memory a thousand times each day when it recurs to thee! Disclaim! disclaim! disclaim! doth it so greatly help thy memory to forget me? Then, since thy memory is a desert, I'll burst upon it like a water-spout and fill all its dried-up rivers to o'erflowing. Thou didst murder me!

Wal. I did not murder thee.

Ghost. Not as a highwayman shoots his victim dead; nor as a midnight robber, with a noiseless blow, crushes the skull of him he'd rob; nor as a burglar, crept thou to my couch with slow and noiseless tread, sinking a dagger in my heart; nor yet with nerve-destroying poison, as thou didst send thy wife to heaven, a short hour ago. With none of these base and cold-blooded, yet quick death means didst thou take me off. But thou didst murder me a million times ere thou wouldst let me die. Know me not yet by this description of my murder? 'Tis no wonder, since thou hast done so many! Dost thou require my name? then I will give it thee. I am Florence Morton—"sweet Flora," as thou used to call me when with honey words thou didst embalm my heart.

[*Enter the ghosts of a man and woman behind* WOLFORD.]

Wol. Oh! let me go from this accursed place. [*As he turns he confronts ghosts.*]

Ghost of man. Ho! villain, thy path for once is blocked.

Wol. Make way or I will kill thee.

Ghost of man. Thou didst that years ago. We are the husband and the wife that thou didst tear asunder on this earth, come back to haunt thy way and make thee die a thousand deaths of fear.

[*Enter ghost of* MIRIAM WOLFORD, *with an orange in her hand.*]

Wol. I will get out of this damned hole! [*Turns to flee and is confronted by ghost of his wife.*]

Ghost. It is an orange of a very peculiar kind, from South America. Will you eat it? You will find it very sweet, but therein lies its peculiar excellence.

Wol. Furies of hell, art thou turned loose upon me? [*Exeunt ghosts.*] Give me more blood! My soul calls out for blood! Give me a battle—a million 'gainst me—that I may drown myself in gore! I'll be a king spite of all gods and men—a king more bloody than was e'er writ of.

CURTAIN.

ACT V.

Scene 1—*Washington—A Room.*

Enter Brandon *and* General Shelborn.

Bra. Are you sure, Shelborn, you have everything prepared in your department?

Shel. Have no fear for the army. It will obey the commands of its chief officer.

Bran. But have you studied well to know on what officers of under-rank you can depend? Are you sure there are no traitors in your council?

Shel. None that I have approached. I have only spoken to those inferior officers upon whom I could with certainty depend. For the obedience of the rest, the commands of their chief shall stand sponser.

Bran. What say you to the valiant Pitsborough? Is he of common mind with us?

Shel. I have not broken the matter to him. I was afraid he would not listen to it with a willing ear.

Bran. I like the General well, and he has always shown regard for me. Yet I am by no means certain of him. He is a man of most predominate influence with the army. The soldiers swear by him. He could work mighty mischief, and the thought grows on me that he is no good man to have against us. Have you done anything to counteract his force in case he turns against us?

Shel. I have not waited for him to show himself against us, but, so to speak it, have nipped him in the bud; given strict orders for his imprisonment with the issuance of the first Imperial proclamation.

Bran. A wiser course could not have been pursued. Listen, Shelborn! Since we have undertaken this enterprise, stop not at trifles in its accomplishment. Make his imprisonment death, if necessary, and so with all others like him. Have you massed all the army here in Washington?

Shel. Every available man.

Bran. And you have at your command?

Shel. Twenty thousand, besides officers.

Bran. If they obey commands, it is enough to put down any rabble. Shelborn, upon the first day's work depends our enterprise. Losing it, I would not give a farthing for our chances; gaining it, have no fear for the morrow. And thus you see, success hangs on your shoulders. Do well your part, and you shall be General-in-Chief of all our armies. And, mark you, Shelborn, they shall not be the striplings they now are, but mighty legions, against which the world could not contend. And with this high position, thou shalt have supplemented a Dukedom. Fear not at using force! Let not blood deter you. What were a river of the red stuff to our future greatness. Men must die, anyway. Forget not the full force and effect of grape-shot. Nothing so cures a mob as well-directed shots of grape. Go now, I pray you, to the head-quarters of the army, and when the inauguration's over, fill the streets with troops, surround the capitol, where we shall be, and strike terror where opposition shows itself. (*Exit Shel.*)

My star has never dimmed. Yet would my mind feel more at ease if that great dream had but concluded differently. What, Brandon, wouldst thou be deterred by phantasies?

Enter WOLFORD.

My brave companion, my great advisor, my more than brother, good morning to you.

Wol. If it is not too soon, how fares Your Majesty?

Bran. Ah! Clarence, thou needst never call me majesty; nor need thy tongue to me speak any title; nor bend thy knee nor bow thy head before me; nor pay me homage; nor do any act to indicate I am above thee. In all respects thou art my perfect equal. We'll be a double king; and I shall lean on thee as a maiden on her lover, and ask thy counsel in every act. Call me but Mentor, as in times gone by; and to me make thy approaches as a friend to one he loves and fears not. Then if in all my kingdom there is aught that thou woulst have—any high title or honorable position—take it without my leave, for I have given it thee already.

Wol. There is a time when gratitude reaches beyond the power of words; when it becomes a silent and unspeakable feeling of the soul. I have heard it said that love exists only between man and woman. But 'tis a lie! For never did man love woman, nor woman man, as I love thee. My affection for thee is deep-rooted, like a mighty mountain, and neither storm nor flood can move it. It is as wide as the great ocean.

Bra. No mountain, even were it made of solid gold, nor the great ocean, holds dearer treasures than my love holds thine.

Wol. I thank thee, Mentor, for thy kind expression; and since thou wilt not let me call thee by any name becoming the royal purple of thy station, then will I call thee brother, that my bonds of fealty may be twice strengthened.

Bra. 'Tis a dear name, and well I like to hear thee call me such. But, Clarence, if I am not too slow of speech to say it now, I thought I saw a greater look of care upon thy face than there was wont to dwell upon it. A lesser friend might not have noticed it. What is it, Clarence; hast thou had some trouble; left you New York last night?

Wol. 'Tis nothing, brother, unless perhaps the coming of this most momentous occasion has caused me loss of sleep in thinking how I might better serve thee.

Bra. My noble friend! And hast thou any great advice to tender me this morning? What are thy thoughts?

Wol. This shall most likely be a bloody day.

Bra. But one renowned in history.

Wol. Doubly would it be renowned if without blood our end could be accomplished.

Bra. Why, so it would; yet we can scarcely hope for that. The quick announcement of our strong determination will doubtless cause excitement. Some rattle-brained idiot will cry "To arms!" and a street struggle will ensue between our royal army and the rabble.

Wol. Have you reckoned on a course if the army should be overcome, or, what is worse, desert you? 'Tis an unpleasant thought, I know, yet sometimes the course of wisdom is not through Andalusian arbors.

Bra. Such contingencies have occurred to me. Indeed, they have been dunning me constantly, and demanding my answer; but like a disagreeable creditor, I have been putting them off until it were no longer the part of statesmanship to do so. Mean as are these possibilities, let us meet them squarely face to face. What wouldst thou suggest, Wolford?

Wol. A remedy most easy. Knowest thou the course that's most direct to the common heart?

Bran. Why, now, I think I'll take thy answer.

Wol. The road runs without by-ways from the pocket.

Bran. And still I think I do not fully understand thee.

Wol. This nation's saddled with an enormous debt, which, twist and turn it as you may, the poor man pays.

Bran. That it is, rather than that it should be so, I think, is true political economy.

Wol. For many years the public clamor has gone up for riddance from this debt.

Bran. And so the people should be rid of it.

Wol. It is now owing to a few men, who, by the foulest means, have merged it in themselves, that they may live in luxury, while the people starve to pay them.

Bran. Too true! Too true! But how shall this assist in the maintenance of our position?

Wol. Wouldst thou be a popular as well as a great king?

Bran. Right well I'd like the approbation of my subjects.

Wol. Then mark me this! When the rabble howls against thee to-day; screeches of liberty o'erthrown; of freedom buried; when demagogues from every public place, with hair disheveled and arms thrown wildly out, tell of our great forefathers' blood that was poured out upon the fields of Lexington and Bunker's Hill, and by such means attempt to raise the masses 'gainst thee—if thou wouldst turn their bitter curses into sweet words of praise for thee, and hear them shout: Long live the King! Long live Ulysses! issue, as thy first Imperial stroke, this edict: The Government is changed, and the debt of the old Government is abolished!

Bran. Thy argument sounds well. But would not such a course bring down dishonor both upon the nation and myself?

Wol. Where is that love, which, but a moment since, came so like molten lava from thy heart, if thou dost think I would advise thee to thy own dishonor?

Bran. Forgive me, Clarence; I know thou would'st not.

Wol. Now, thou speakest like my brother. As to the *nation*, there shall no longer be a nation. That which was shall be thy kingdom, thy imperial realm, and rests there any obligations on thee to pay the debts thy uncle left in dying?

Bran. My worthiest counsellor, thy course shall be adopted.

Wol. 'Tis thy course, Brandon, not mine. I would have thee have all the honor of it; therefore, speak of it to no man, till after thou hast done it, and then the people will hold up their hands and say, Behold the wisdom and the justice of our king!

Bran. Thou would'st sacrifice anything for me, Clarence. Now that I cast my eye across the plain of our great undertaking, as we near the Mecca, I see thou hast made thyself a dray-horse for me. Had it not been for thee I would have stalled in the sands before I started. I can never pay thee for all thy help.

Wol. No more! no more!

Bran. Then wait thee here till our great coadjutors come, while I attend for a little while some personal preparations for the great event. [*Exit* BRAN.]

Wol. My horse is saddled and my armor's on; now will he ride me swiftly to the crown. Come, thou sweet money instruments, till I attune thee to accord with me.

Enter RANDEMER, STARLOW, *an Admiral, and a number of others.*

Good morning, my lords, dukes, earls, viscounts, barons, marquises, to be. How fare ye all on this great gala day? Upon a fairer day than this the sun ne'er shone, and in the eve go down upon a royal throne!

Ran. Our friend seems in a royal mood this morning.

Wol. And why should I not be, when all the signs are so propitious? Does the farmer sigh at a bright day in haying-time?

Ran. Rather I would ask: Does a railroad man cry when the Legislature adjourns?

Wol. I admit the simile is a better one. But now to the matters of the times. This day is likely to be one that will try men's souls. Are you sure of all the railroads?

Ran. Have no fear for them.

Wol. What say you of the navy, my Lord Admiral?

Admiral. I may say you need have no fear of that, either; it is very harmless.

Wol. The army, under General Shelborn is ours—so, what need we fear? Our ends are all accomplished before we begin.

Star. Why, so they are. Most largely owing to our great adviser, head-and-front, Wolford.

Wol. The noble Earl of California flatters me! Why do we want this change of government? Why do we want a king? Can you tell me, Starlow?

Star. In few words. I want no more of rabbles; no more strikes; no more talk of confiscation; no more blackmailing. In short, I want my property protected.

Wol. Quite rightly answered. And what say you, Randemer?

Ran. In addition to what my friend from California says, I want to feel that I can go to bed at night and wake up in the morning without feeling that, in the meantime, a law has been passed prohibiting the payment of my Government bonds—or, what is just as bad, paying them in greenbacks.

Wol. So you are right. This is the idea predominant: Stability in property rights; above all the prompt and faithful payment of the principal and interest of our national debt. In other words, the maintenance of our country's honor unspotted. A king who would not do this is worse than no king at all.

Ran. For my part, I'd raise my hand as quickly to dethrone him as I now do to set up noble Brandon.

Wol. Most noble Brandon! (Aside.) Most noble Brandon.

SCENE 2.—*A street in Washington. A number of Citizens around a bulletin-board.*

Enter GENERAL PITSBOROUGH.

Pits. I wonder what means all this excitement? Some great event must have happened. I will see. [Goes up to board.] A proclamation! Can I believe my eyes? Brandon has proclaimed himself Emperor! This is no time for thoughts, but actions. Citizens, know you what that means? Are you struck dumb?

Cit. What does it mean? I cannot see to read it.

Pits. What does it mean? That you are no longer sovereigns, but subjects; no longer freemen, but slaves; that liberty is dead; that ye have a king, that Brandon has proclaimed himself Emperor! To arms, citizens, to arms, and let no traitor live! Redeem your land from tyrants! By your blood redeem it!

Cits. To arms! To arms!

Enter four guards.

1st Guard. General Pitsborough, I have a warrant for your arrest.

Pits. What villainy is this? (*Snatches warrant and reads.*) "His Royal Majesty, Ulysses I., Emperor of America, sends greeting." His Royal Majesty, Ulysses I., Emperor, be damned! Take back that greeting to him. Tell him I know him not. This is America, my own free land, and my duty is to no sovereign save the Constitution and my country's flag. (*Grinds warrant under his feet.*)

1st Guard. Help, guards! take hold of him; he destroys the warrant. (*Guards take hold of* PITS.)

Pits. Let go me, traitors, or, by the gods, I'll carve your hearts out! (*Draws his sword, and, while struggling with Guards*—)

Enter Company of U. S. Army.

Capt. What, ho! who dares to treat my senior thus? (*Rushes at Guards with his sword, when they let go of* PITS. *and flee.*)

Pits. I thank you, Captain. Which way go you with your company? Why are you here?

Capt. Surely, I know not, General, save as an order bade me to patrol the streets and quell all riots and disturbances.

Pits. Know you that Brandon has proclaimed himself Emperor?

Offs. and Sols. What!

Pits. 'Tis so; there is the royal edict. And those fellows that ye saw had a warrant for my arrest, signed by His Royal Majesty, Ulysses I.

Capt. Outrageous!

Pits. Oh, ye old war-stained veterans! some of ye marched with me under the stars and stripes full many a thousand miles, braved sickness, death and prison, to hold this country one.

Sols. So we did, General.

Pits. Marched ye to the cannon's belching mouth: gave ye your fathers, brothers, sons: left ye your mothers, wives and sisters: did ye all this to make a royal cradle of your country? a breeding-nest for tyrants—a hatching-house for kings, and dukes and earls ?

Sols. That we didn't.

Pits. Loyal sons of freedom, who never knew the tyranny of kingly rule, for which will ye choose to fight—to make Brandon Emperor, or for your homes, your liberty, and for your country?

Sols. Home, liberty and country.

Pits. Then follow me, and neither eat, nor drink, nor sleep, till every traitor's head lies at your feet. Up, citizens! Break open armories, gun-shops; bring out your arms and fight, for liberty is assaulted. Save it or die. On to the capital, where we may strike the traitors!

[*They start to march, when enter* GENERAL SHELBORN, *with a company of U. S. army.*]

Shel. (to Pits.) Why are you here? There is a warrant for your arrest. Arrest him, soldiers.

Pits. Nay, arrest me not!

Shel. Will you obey me, then? I am your senior.

Pits. Thou art a traitor, and I know no senior now, save God, the Constitution and my flag. Charge, company.

[They fight off the stage.]

Enter an OLD MAN, *followed by citizens carrying all sorts of arms.*

Old Man. Full seventy years ago this gun did serve me and my country, under Jackson, at Orleans. But this old palsied body and flint-lock are not too old to fight for freedom yet.

Enter Company of U. S. Army.

Be ye loyal to America, or fight ye for a king?

Capt. Long live the king!

Old Man. Short life to ye! [Shoots him. Fight between Citizens and Soldiers.]

[*Between the second and third scenes the battle should be heard continuously, and the scenery shifted with all possible despatch.*

SCENE 3——*Washington. A room in the Capitol; present,* BRANDON *as Emperor, in state costume,* WOLFORD, RANDEMER, STARLOW *and others, dressed in the style of the present nobility of Europe, while at court. The noise of a battle rages without.*

Enter an AID-DE-CAMP.

Bran. What news bring you from your General?

Aid. That the battle is still raging.

Ran. (to Aid.) Say Your Majesty!

Aid. Your Majesty!

Bran. A deaf man would have known that. What says he of the battle?

Aid. That he is fighting with all his might, Your—Your Majesty.

Bran. Fool! What said he of the result?

Aid. That he was wounded four times, Your—Your Excellency—Your Majesty, I mean.

Wol. How runs the battle, idiot?

Aid. My Lord—Your Majesty—the General bid me say that three-fourths of all the soldiers have deserted to Pitsborough, who leads the patriots—I mean the rebels, and that the citizens have possession of all the arms in the city, and that he cannot hold out ten minutes longer, and for you to flee for your lives.

Bran. Go back to your General, and tell him that it is my royal command that he fight it out on this line if it takes all summer.

Aid. (retiring—aside.) I don't think it will take that long, Your—your what-you-may-call-it-old-idiot! [*Exit.*

Wol. (to Brandon.) Your Majesty will hear better news when he you sent to tell of the abolition of the national debt, comes back.

Enter MESSENGER, *with clothes torn.*

Bran. Your looks import no good; but blurt it out.

Mess. Your Majesty, when I began to speak to the citizens, they, thinking that I was one of them, all gave attentive ear. But when I told them what my mission was, and scattered the royal proclamation 'mongst them, they said: "What will he"—they used worse terms, Your Majesty.

Bran. Damn the terms!—what said they?

Mess. "What, will he not only steal the government, and rob us of our liberties, but must he also blacken the nation's honor and repudiate her debts?" And then they fell upon me, and I had to flee for my life.

Ran. What is it I hear? What said you to them, that they said this?

Mess. My lord, when I proclaimed to the citizens, by order of His Majesty, that the national debt had been abolished by His Royal Majesty's imperial edict, it was then the citizens said as I have told you.

Star. A royal edict abolishing the national debt! Is this so, your Majesty?

Bran. It is, my noble lord.

Ran. Do you hear that, my lords? What think you of it? We make a king that our property might be protected, and by his first imperial act, save that the people stopped him, he would have robbed us of half our wealth!

Bran. Dare you speak of me in that manner? I am the King and my royal will is law.

Ran. Gods! I like not that kind of a king.

Lords. Nor I! Nor I!

Ran. We will not have him, either! We will have a king that will protect our property.

Lords. We will not have him.

Bran. My lords, silence! I will have you all imprisoned.

Ran. Imprisoned? Where is your power? Down from that royal station thou hast disgraced! [*Lords draw swords and start for* BRANDON.] Down, or we'll kill thee! [BRANDON *comes down.*]

Star. There is no time for parley. Let us select a King who will be a King. Lord Wolford is my choice.

Ran. So is he mine; he will protect our property.

Lords. And mine.

Ran. As there is no dissent, Lord Wolford, we hail thee as our Majesty.

Bra. Would you, Clarence?

Wol. If so it be the will of you, most noble gentlemen, that I assume the heavy cares of state at this most pressing moment, I consent. [Ascends throne.]

Bra. Oh, Wolford! if from all the millions of this earth I had had but one choice of a friend, it had been thee. Alas! I care not now for human glory.

Wol. My lords, all hope is not yet gone. If we can hold till morning, great Maxwell and McDonald will be here with strong legions.

Enter an Aid-de-camp.

Aid. Your Majesty, a message just received by General Shelborn, which he bade me give thee.

Wol. My Lord of California, will you read it? [Aid gives to Star.]

Star. [reads]. "Maxwell and McDonald both murdered by the mob."

Bra. Maxwell and McDonald dead!

Enter Messenger.

Mess. Your Majesty, Congress has hastily assembled and passed a bill declaring all adherents to Brandon traitors, and confiscating their property.

R. and S. Our railroads confiscated!

Enter MINNARD (*clothes bloody and sword in hand.*]

Wol. Where has your noble lordship been? We have not seen thee all day.

Min. Where I had hoped to find thee, villain. What! art thou on the throne? Has thou murdered Brandon too?

Wol. He has gone mad, my lords; take charge of him!

Min. Nay, touch me not. The first man dies who dares do so. (Advancing on Wolford.) Fight now, thou murderous traitor; thou false friend; thou cowardly betrayer of my wife and child! Fight, or I'll put my sword through you.

Wol. Away, you petty idiot. I am the king.

Min. I care not if thou art king a million times. I'll have thy blood. Wilt thou not draw thy sword? Coward that thou art, since thou'lt show no fight, I'll kill thee anyway. Take that (stabs him), and that (stabs again). [Wolford dies. Hammering at the door, and great confusion, both in and out of room.]

Mess. Two kings deposed within two minutes! One king a minute. The royal stock will soon run out at that. Gods—I think this is no good country for kings. They'll make me one next. I'll go. [*Exit* MESS.]

Min. (to lords.) Another minute more and the rabble will be upon us. If ye be men, stand, fight and die! If ye be cowards, run for your worthless lives.

[*The door is broken in and Citizens and Soldiers rush in, bearing upon a bayonet the head of* SHELBORN. *Savage shouts.*]

1st Cit. Down with the traitors!

2d Cit. Off with their heads!

[RANDEMER, STARLOW *and some of the lords attempt to escape, but are followed by citizens and soldiers.* MINNARD, BRANDON *and others fight with citizens and soldiers and are overpowered. The citizens and soldiers who have followed* RANDEMER, STARLOW *and others return with heads of same on bayonets.*]

Enter OLD MAN, *wounded.*

Old Man. Now can I die, since I have seen the severed heads of the last American nobility. [*Dies.*]

Enter GENERAL PITSBOROUGH.

Pits. Citizens, soldiers, patriots all: You have preserved your sacred liberties. The spirit of your fathers, in you, is not dead. 'Twas slumbering, but now 'tis roused to sleep no more. Nourish it; protect it while you live, and dying bequeath it to your children as the richest legacy that you can leave them. (To the audience.) Though this is but a dream of empire, to those with royal aspirations let it also be a warning.

CURTAIN.

www.ingramcontent.com/pod-product-compliance
Lightning Source LLC
Chambersburg PA
CBHW030907260626
47169CB00008B/2733

* 9 7 8 3 3 3 7 1 7 5 6 7 2 *